SUMMER LOVE

(Two Worlds of Emotions Inside)

SUMMER LOVE

(Two Worlds of Emotions Inside)

Oliver Frances

Published by Marco A Diaz at createspace

Copyright 2010 Marco A Diaz

This book is licensed for your personal enjoyment only. This book may not be resold or given away to other people. If you would like to share this book with another person, please purchase an additional copy for each person you share it with. If you're reading this book and did not purchase it, or it was not purchased for your use only, then please return to createspace.com and purchase your own copy. Thank you for respecting the hard work of this author.

Summer Love

I

"I know that it isn't what you want… Definitely, what we got is so great, but we should go on in different ways."

"But, I love you."

Her partner gave her a tired look.

"Don't hold on to me, please. No reason for."

"I love you. And, it is my reason."

"I know… But, I can't go on."

"Isn't it enough for you?" she asked timidly.

"I'm afraid, but…"

"Why?"

"Why!" He told. "We don't understand each other."

"A couple might have problem, but we can sort it out."

Graham came out with bitter words. "Pat, I don't love you. No answer to this. You can't understand it, can you? I don't love you!"

"Perhaps, I am the one… Sometimes, you have to lose something completely to appreciate it."

"Don't be silly! I do not love you. And, I don't want you!"

"No, please… If I have to get on my knees, I will," Pat implored.

"You should accept it. I don't love you!" He bawled, in despair.

Her melancholy countenance made him feel compassion for his lover. "I'm sorry… But, when someone doesn't want to be with the other, the best is part company. Pat, nobody's for good. Sooner or later, you will meet someone else. And, you will love him. You won't die for sure if I walk out on you. No one dies for another."

Summer Love

"Perhaps, I will."

Graham, walking up to the door to leave the place, said. "Don't be such a melodramatic cow. Tomorrow, you'll live like today. You might well not remember the past."

"Bye Pat," told he, without turning around.

She bore in mind this scene like a litany every night before closing her eyes.

II

The lad, strolling over the pebbles with a folded deck chair in his left hand, contemplated the different multicoloured sails that traversed the broad sea thrust by the intense current of air. He, marvelling at the splendour of the tones of the sea, had continued pacing up to the westwards of the beach.

"Busy?" He asked to the blonde woman, seated down near.

"No."

Unfolding the seat and covering it with a towel, he rested himself on it to begin enjoying the fulgent sun.

"Been here for long?" Kenny told shyly.

"About half an hour."

To continue with the initiated dialogue, she said. "What do you do?"

"I'm attending a postgraduate course in Advertising at Watford at the moment. And, I do something else in my free time," answered the guy, astounded at her first question.

"Such as?"

"I'm writer."

The brief silence was broken when he questioned her. "What do you do?"

"I'm pathologist. By the way, have you got any work produced?"

"Not yet."

Keeping the thread of the chat, Kenny added. "Where do you work?"

"At University College Hospital, but I will quit there soon. A friend and I have got plans to start our own business this year. I hope that everything will go right… Always, everybody has got so many plans for a year that in the end they get nowhere."

Summer Love

The lady, reclining in the deck chair, closed her eyes to raise her conscience to the sense of the huge pleasure that was given by the gilt sunbeams that suffused every part of her body.

In that moment, Kenny felt an enormous sort of desire that enraptured him, and it was not more than going on communicating with that special person. By words, he would know more about this woman that delighted his soul. Thus would be satisfied his eagerness yet greater.

Retaking the conversation, the lad affirmed. "It is just a chance to have met us here in the south."

"Well, you can say it again… I enjoy seeing the sea."

"So do I."

Kenny's vision wandered upon greenish waters while reasoning on how he should deal with this lady. An abominable repudiation was produced to act as he has done many times before, where a different personality blossomed like the most precious flower in spring rather than his own to attract the person wished. It was a foolish position! But, it was the same attitude as many people assume towards what they consider important, if there is something relevant in this life. He had represented that role like an actor in a drama for having felt inferior or tried to get a little part of that which was sought. Now, everything was distinct because it was felt the need of proceeding in a different manner. And, it was not more than showing his true colours.

"I like to admire the sea -a way of calming myself down… One completely joyride since I had to take the train to come down! I was crazy to be near the coast."

"A bit crazy there... in the city. By the way, I can drive you up to London."

"Then, I won't hitchhike," she accepted, jesting.

Bedazzled by the beauty of those limpid green eyes, the lad told. "You are so gorgeous that it would be very difficult for anyone to describe you."

"Thanks." It was the only response to one of the compliments that the lady had listened to from the chap.

On the motorway, half way in direction towards the city, a pocket black device went off. Drawing it out of her satchel, Pat heard the message.

"Already, it's started to call me, although I said that I would arrive in London about seven o' clock."

"Don't think that I am going to gather speed."

"Oh... No! Don't worry. You don't have to hurry up."

"I like speed but won't put my foot down. I want to have more time with you,' Kenny said to please her still more.

A few blocks away from Pat's home, he asked. "Can I have your number?"

"Well, you know where to meet me again."

Casualness took an important role one more time. The possibility of bumping into her person would be wagered on it. A negative response was hinted. Perhaps, it was better than a false promise. He had failed again. Why? It seems that there was no explanation for it.

"Would you want to jot down my number?"

Opening a rectangular leather purse wallet to delve into it for a piece of paper, she announced. "I'm afraid, I haven't got a pen."

Summer Love

Kenny, casting his eyes quickly over the small folding case, noticed a ballpoint pen in a side of it.

I tried. It's better not to insist; he considered.

"Have my card," offered the lady suddenly.

Minutes later, the lad dropped her off. Entering her lonely apartment, she came into her bedroom to undress and have a shower. After, Pat slipped into pale colours and went out to the living room.

The apricot coloured light of a summer day came through the panes of window and suffused the place. She did not want to have meal, so that, flinging herself down into the sofa, Pat observed the room for a space of some minutes. Meanwhile her eyelids became as heavy as lead, and, in a doze, she began to think. In the near future, the litany that scourged and hurt her deeply would disappear. Everything would be totally distinct. It was her perception. The senses indicate that the young had not approached to gain anything from her. He was quite different from the others, who had met in her life. In this moment, many questions gave rise about this someone who had appeared in the course of her life. Who was he? Where had he been? Why did she come across him at this moment? All of them were irrelevant questions. The only significant thing was that Kenny was interested in her, though. He was not the one that Pat had wished to be. At any rate, she was drawn to him and made herself forget the unpleasant experiences of the past. It seemed to be an illusion. Or, was just a dream? Perhaps, it was one dream of becoming liberated of the oppression of the chains of unpleasant memories. At last! She would be free. And, the release meant a sensation of

Summer Love

enthusiasm which was nearly to

blossom out inside her.

III

Two weeks had gone by after that Sunday, when Kenny, with a sort of hesitation characteristic of his personality, decided to phone her up. His nervous fingers dialled one of the numbers impressed on the card. Unexpectedly, a message came out on the line from an automatic operator indicating the failure in the system by the number. A thrill of annoyance ran through him because of that. However, his listless fingers attempted the other numbers. But, he was not able to be in touch with Pat.

Kenny, dropping himself on the wood veneer telephone seat, began to consider that an obstacle appeared not to let him grasp what he most desired as in many occasions in the past. It may be better to forget her. And, this was the convenient moment for it. But, the lad could not renounce the emotion that represented the lady. It was a sort of ardour that had made him conscious of he was a being made out of flesh and blood. Pat had given back the emotion necessary for life, because without it we would be beings lacking in grace.

Nonetheless, Kenny didn't convince himself so that he tried the contact number of her pager again. And this time, there was no any problem at all.

A mysterious dread started up all her senses highly as the lad's number appeared on the little screen. He meant an unknown temptation to which the lady had never yielded. This time would she cede to it? What implications would it have? Nothing would be learnt if she did not go for it. One always believes to have the knowledge about an experience from outside. This conviction taints our judgments and brings equivocal resolutions. No one can understand a reality if she or he is not involved in it. Those reflections emanated from her mind like innumerable ideas from a writer's before his work.

Giving a thought about it, Pat had expected to have some determination meanwhile she was seated on a stool in the laboratory. However, no idea crossed her mind. Time went by, and nothing struck her. To discover what was to be the right decision, the call had to be made. She gathering up her courage dialled his home number.

A half an hour later the telephone rang, Kenny -not being aware of the person that could be phoning- lifted the receiver carelessly. As the lady's voice was heard an expression of astonishment came over his face. Speaking nervously, both them had a short dialogue useful to agree to meet one another at the weekend.

IV

Kenny contemplated with exquisite marvel and in silence the figure of the lady that was laid on a towel over the pebbles. His view wended from her fine-moulded long limbs up to her nymph-like petite bosom falling on her sparkling eyes, whilst his thought was bemused inasmuch as the discernment of the fact of that he was living a romantic passion or another sort of emotion that may be confused with love. But, there was no hesitation in his soul.

Summer Love

Definitely he was in love. And, this was not mere sentiment. Indeed, simple love belongs to shallow people.

To him, the lady was similar to a model that defines lines of a renovated school to an artist. Fascination was an emotion that bloomed inside him –Kenny had not yet discovered it by himself. And, she provoked charm over his person too. The beautiful being was something so perfect that she ought not to be touched just to be perceived by membranes of the sight.

"Life is tough and you've got two paths by which you can go for the thing you desire. The first, one of the easiest and the implication is to leave moral principles and scruples. The second, you can define it as the hardest way because it requires sacrifice. The reward given by the last one is the following rule: the thing so difficult to get is the one that for longer you can have in your hands. Everything comes and goes," said Pat, and sat on the deck chair.

"Temptations always come along and, I guess these mean accepting situations or doing things that through a moral point of view are not considered as good actions.

Anyway, the most desired thing seems to be reached through immoral actions. But, I am not the guy used to getting a thing by vicious means. Perhaps, the world thinks that it is silly, but I don't think so."

"Remember this rule: if you get something easy you won't keep it long. Anything that has a bad beginning will have a bad end," she assured him.

"In my experience, I realize that you must wait until the precise moment to achieve your aims. I mean, until every element concerned with the whole thing is favourable. You can work so hard for anything, but if the factors are not positive, you won't succeed. On the other hand, if you don't concentrate on something because it has been left, you will get it without too much effort.

A sense of dissatisfaction came over her.

"I don't think so. If you do the impossible you get anything you want."

"But, all elements have to be in your favour."

"You gotta work for that," muttered the young lady.

The lad perceived the long distance between each other, in spite of being so close to her. This was conveyed by his friend's sound voice, which mirrored a certain sort of boundary inside her and outside. He came across a barrier to defeat in order to become involved in her life.

Kenny expecting that the woman realized about his sentiments told. "You're so charming… I can't think of something else. And, it is a huge pleasure to be by your side."

"Don't say more compliments, please."

"I like doing it."

"I hope that you don't go around saying compliments."

It was not expected such explanation owing to the lack of reason for it. The lad's polite expression was intended to have an effusive manifestation of affect, which could have been through pleasant words or body language. His intention was not accomplished. His senses were not satisfied even though she was just deemed sacred and untouchable. Words had to annihilate the frustration.

"How is your work going?" He asked listlessly.

"Too much... and, it's still more because I am so busy with the establishment of my company. What about you?"

The nuisance was intensified more as he was reminded of a theme that distressed his mind. In that moment of pleasure, the dissatisfaction had one place.

"I've had some problems with the publisher, because I need to cover part of the cost of the publication."

"A great deal?"

"Yes, when you are short of money anything asked is a good deal. With this money I guess that I could make a trip. And, I would invite you."

Summer Love

"I would accept the invitation unless my work let me go."

Those words delimited any sort of relation.

Kenny, perched over the upper part of the deck chair with his back to her, observed the ample greenish waters as he was lost in the depth of his meditations. The lady may well have been like the sea that was in front of his eyes. Who could know if her demeanour was similar to its waves that move to and fro incessantly? What if her behaviour was the same? It was not actually relevant. Everybody is a sea. Tenebrous

Summer Love

moments identical to troubled water involve us seeming about to linger for ages, as in hours our person lives frenzied emotions as if they were amidst a whirlpool. And, after any adventure, our souls fall surrendered, appearing to be calm currents as the gale ceased.

    Her personality was considered so important. And, what about his? What was he like? In that instant, the lad realized about another small detail of life in this adventure. He had forgotten himself -identically to everybody. This let him comprehend that each was similar to the other, even though we exert to believe that one is completely different from another.

There was no other way... He had just to embark himself on that vessel which would drift on her sea, where his mettle might wreck owing to the strong currents. If he could arrive at the other coast a dream named under the title of happiness would be awaiting him.

"You should be like a guardian angel, Pat," said the young, hinting a possible relationship.

Once more she called to his mind the advice that he must take it into account emphasizing. "If my work lets me."

Kenny turned her disagreeable expression into the most precious words.

"It'll be beautiful... so when you have a little bit of free time you'll spend it with me."

"It'll be so."

At last, he drew out from her curved red lips delightful words to his person.

That night, Pat, when lay sleepless, on her ample bed adorned with blue French accessories matching the curtains and the D-ring canopy

Summer Love

and the cover of another item of furniture, in her bedroom perfumed with a pot-pourri of delightful fragrances of aromatic mixtures of exotic flowers and herbs and oils; thought about the enthusiasm that her life had got over. Innumerable sentiments had flourished in her soul again. The lad had rejuvenated her changing the colours of her life defined by chiaroscuro into a variety of brilliant tones. Her recollection of his person was present in her life, though. It was not love.

In amidst those emotions came along one stronger hidden in a part of the human soul and too impossible to be recognized. That sensation was one that turned into a phantom and pursued our frenzied desires until paralysed our deeds. And, it was not more that dread -which she felt enormously. Kenny's youth represented a horrible fear. The days of profound anxiety and depression became in the past, in spite of the fact that there was no favourable sign that deleted the failure in her destiny. In her reflections was not considered that he had been the person who had saved her from remaining into the abyss where her life was.

Summer Love

Now, it was impossible not to fall asleep. Any consideration would be better to be left for the following dawn. The fresh morning air would help her to meditate about the things that crossed her mind.

Summer Love

V

The afternoon light smote the white place at Hampstead.

Kenny excited walked up and down like a being caged. From a cup, which had in a hand, he sipped lemon tea meanwhile thought about what fate had in store for him.

"I don't know what it's going to happen," said he languidly.

The brainless charwoman with rugged features and clumsy in movements represented the perfect which listen to our deeds without reproaching them. She beheld the guy as foreseeing a comment -which he had not made yet.

Before his lips began to pronounce any word, the shrill voice asked. "Why 're you saying it with so much pity?"

"I can't explain it… It's like a foreboding. Something tells me that I'll have trouble and… it means the loss of that which I desire enormously."

"Why?"

"I don't know how to deal with the situation. In fact, nothing's been said. We keep moving around the point."

"Don't lose your hair. Wait and see."

Kenny, sitting down on one of the chairs at the table -close to the kitchen area, observed the bricked patio through the panes of the hardwood door that were not covered with sheer curtains.

"Wait! I've done it many times. I'm always waiting… I fear to fail again. The worst is coming I can see in front of my eyes."

Summer Love

"Why everything has to go wrong?" The handmaid asked, shrieking out.

"Why not? There is no reason for everything to go right. When you wish something too much, you can assure that you won't reach that thing. That always occurs. If you don't care about it, you'll have it."

"How can know that the worst is coming if it hasn't happened so far?"

"I merely perceive it."

VI

In one afternoon, Pat along with Kate walked over the grey linoleum floor of the lifeless passage, whose dim illumination made the colour of the walls imperceptible for human eyes. In the middle of the corridor, awaiting one of the lifts, their bodies felt a chilly draught that streamed through the place. As the steel doors opened, a friend of theirs got out of the shaft.

"If we don't bump into you here, you forget us," told Kate.

"I've been so busy with the arrangement of the wedding that I haven't got any time for myself."

"Are you getting married?" Pat asked, startled.

"I haven't said to you that Caroline is getting married?"

"No."

"A month away from today, exactly," the bride announced smiling. "Are you going to have lunch?"

"Yes," Kate answered.

"Then, I'll see you at Fitzroy. I'm sorry not to keep you company right now, but I have to speak to Dr.

Goldstone before he leaves the hospital."

They entered a little pale green room and took seats at a round table.

"Pat, we have to hurry up to register the name of the company and look for a place where the lab will operate."

"I'm blacked out at the present."

"Are you... What bugs you?" Kate questioned. "Don't tell me that Graham got back."

"I feel nothing for him anymore."

"Are you sure, Pat?"

Contemplating the passers by along the alley through the huge windows before them, she assured her friend. "Absolutely."

"Have you met somebody else?"

A word was murmured from her sensual lips when a café maid, in a green shirt and black trousers, brought the lunches to them.

"Then, you've told me nothing."

"What do you want to hear, Kate?" Pat said, with vivacious eyes.

"I would like to find out the reason that makes you lose your head. It should be exciting that you don't know where you are. Delightful! I envy you. Could you tell me? Or, I am not your friend anymore to know about it?"

"Yes, you are… and, since a long time ago."

The conversation was interrupted once more. This time, it was by Caroline who showed up with her fiancé.

Immediately Pat thought of the lad who was enamouring her as she saw the figure of a mature man who would be the spouse of her friend. It must be such a long time until she and the youngster reached that stage of the human being's life, if their relationship

Summer Love

led to a marriage. But, he was too young to consider an eternal union. That lady who was her colleague could aspire to get married since she was delivering her life up to a contemporary man. All her illusion was an absurdity or, perhaps, madness. It had been a folly. She had behaved similarly to an adolescent to have dreams about desires that were out of reality. The youth are those who yearn for the unattainable whilst the elder resign to what life set at their reach. Many times, she had wondered about the reason of such conduct -but figuring it out unsuccessfully. It was

Summer Love

not a riddle. The unique explanation was that people did the most stupid things for the noblest motives.

"Can you tell me your address, Pat? Patrizzia! Are you well, girl?" Caroline asked, with a diary in one hand to write down the response.

"What do you say?" Pat said, paying attention to her friend.

"I'd better give it to you for her," offered Kate.

As the couple left the place, one asked another. "Pat, what is wrong with you? Your mind was wondering when Caroline was here. Sincerely, something must be happening to you. Can't you tell me?"

Not giving any importance to her absentmindedness, she excused herself. "My mind was in someone place else. Don't bother yourself about it. Perhaps, I am a little bit mad these days."

"Mad about anyone?"

"Being absurd about someone," said Pat, growing sad.

From that moment, Kenny lost any possibility of possessing the lady, who before accepted his person with a sort of reluctance. From now on, the lad would have her absolute disdain to

Summer Love

all his considerations. The only thing that would be left was the hope in his soul, which may well be lost before her indifference.

VII

The dark blue car drew up on the narrow cracked pavement outside of one abandoned home, in whose façade rubbish was piled up. The atmosphere was miserable. By the dreary and long Fernandale Rd, from time to time, grotesque and some hostile-faced passers-by walked along and drunken men were hanging around.

The tall figure of a slim man got out of the car. Passing by the dingy and peeled off painted houses, he strolled down up to the apartment buildings. The coldness of the area was so impressing that it annoyed him for a while. Leaving behind the car park between the constructions, he stepped into the building where the flat was which he would call on.

His coarse fingers hammered the door.

"Who is it?"

"Pat?"

"Yes, it's me. Who are you?"

"Graham."

After her ear drums vibrated by the sound of the words that mentioned his name, a shiver went all over and a blank look came on her countenance. Every throb of her heart accelerated, and she was left motionless. In a curious way, Pat experienced it since her sense could not recognize the familiar voice.

The rage was a sort of blaze that flared up inside her as the colour came back to her cheeks.

"What have you come here for?" She spluttered.

"To talk to you," answered her ex-lover, in such a tranquil way.

"I think that we have nothing to talk about."

"You don't have anything to say, but I myself need to speak to you. If you don't open the door, I'll knock until you are fed up with the noise."

Stepping into the living room, Graham greeted the old lady that was sat down in the couch.

"How are you, Mrs. Mary?"

"Well. It's been long time since we heard anything from you," she mumbled leaving the place with leaden steps.

Being discourteous, Pat asked. "What do you want?"

He flung himself down on the arm of a chair beside the sofa to begin the conversation.

"How is it going?"

"Get to the point, please."

Graham frowned in signal of hesitation.

"Sincerely, I don't know how to begin," said he, giggling. "I came here 'cause I have something to tell, but finding myself here now, I have a lot of difficulty in saying, at least, a word… I know that I behaved like a rat. But, when I left you… I have to admit that I went for affairs. I realized that the person that satisfied me in all senses was the one who I pushed away. Many times, I wanted to get back to you, but I didn't dare because I was afraid of your response. Any emotion that I lived intensely didn't help me to forget you. So, I decided to come to you."

Seated opposite her ex-partner, she exploded in cholera. "You know how painful it was to see you going through that door! And, how did I beg you not to leave me?"

"Pat, I know... What did you want me to do? Everything was very confusing then... and I thought leaving was the best. You didn't want to do it, for that reason I behaved as I did."

"And why didn't you realize it before?" She cried out.

"I ain't Mr. Right."

"Time has gone by since you left me, and now you want me to understand your mistakes. Why should I have to make a fool of myself? Or, do I have to be grateful for your return? You wish I took pity on you. Who takes pity on me? I must on others, but nobody on me. I don't know what I have done to deserve this! Tell me, I am so silly?" Pat told as tears welled up in her eyes.

Summer Love

He rose to his feet to go up to his friend to embrace.

"Calm down, I don't want you to say right now that we are going to start over. I just want to let you know I am willing to patch things up. And, I'll do it as long as you let me."

"I don't want to get back to the same situation as before. Honestly, I don't think that I am in love with you anymore."

"Don't say that, please. Just give me a chance."

Freeing herself, Pat asked. "How many times?"

"Just one more."

Summer Love

"I have given you so many... And you have always let me down. What am I going to give you one more for? To disappoint me."

"Now everything is going to be different. Trust me."

"I don't promise anything, but I'll think."

VIII

It seems that people do not remain satisfied in any stirring adventure -yet still if passion is in it, albeit having rejoiced themselves in every moment of it. To go for an exquisite pleasure that one has already had it might well transform a sensation into obsession, whose origin belongs to human nature. If somebody has had the delectation of possessing what was desired, what is the reason by which that person is still attracted to it? The simplest

Summer Love

explanation is that nobody contents with what they have reached.

In fact, they had tasted many sorts of emotions, so that life had nothing in store for them. Her considerations were to accept that they had gone further than the exciting moments in their relationship and the separation was not so disagreeable because it only represented a turn of a page of another chapter of her life. However, such deliberation was not already taken when her ex-partner appeared to disapprove of it.

Summer Love

Lying in her balmy room, Pat meditated on the nature of deeds that occurred through a lifetime. Although every hour went by as if they were similar to air that slipped through the sails of a vessel, her mind was not able to get one resolution to liberate her sentiments from confusion in order to have a pronouncement that mirrored her eagerness. In those crucial moments, the only response meant friendship. It is always presumed that friends are the most convenient people to help us to reinforce our deeds. And, they might be catalogued in two sorts: ones who never mention truth and comfort us with the most delightful eulogies for our person, and the others that confront us to expose realism. Nevertheless, man is always searching for the first ones who are more charming to him.

"You are not going to believe when I tell you who was here on Sunday."

"Perhaps."

"Graham."

"Who... what did he want?" Kate asked, startled.

"To apologize for his behaviour and express his feelings for me. He says that he had realized about his mistakes and wants me to give him another opportunity to patch things up between us."

"Your reaction before it?"

"Anger... After all, I've been disappointed in every chance given to him, and my heart has sunk every time that he has left me in the worst way. And now, he had the nerve to come here to talk about love. How do you want me to react?"

"Yes, you're right."

"I don't still believe that he was here."

"Well, you wish as anyone to have a lasting relationship with the person that you love. And, if Graham is now aware of his mistakes, you can try again."

"Yes."

"Well, what is your intention?" Pat's friend demanded curiously.

"I don't know yet. Before everything was quite different from the present, and I never took anybody else into account. And…"

"Do you think possible to have any relation with the other?"

Putting into words her pessimism, Pat said. "I don't think that it is advisable to encourage any kind of relation in the present conditions.

He is quite young. Besides, he looks like a son of mine."

"And, this is the reason that keeps you away from him?"

"Yes. There's no other. He's marvellous… but, too young."

"I understand. Then, are you going to back to Graham?"

"What would you do in my situation?"

"It's a tricky decision. With one, already you lived a stormy relationship and the other one is an oasis to you."

"I should remind you that one is almost an adolescent," she interrupted her friend.

Summer Love

Apprehending the true signification of those words, Kate suggested. "In my opinion, you should put him behind though it is quite hard for you. I know that the guy made you conceive an illusion and warbled gentle words to your ear -describing amazing emotions that you have never lived with anybody- to raise your ego. Anyway, you should take account of the fact that the relation would not last so long. This is my advice... And, it doesn't mean that you must accept Graham. On the other hand, nobody knows if he is different now. So… to find out you have to try once more."

Summer Love

"What if it is a lie? Go through again! If I had done the same as he did, do you think that he would have turned back? I don't think so. Then, why must I take the risk?"

"You should take it. Besides, it's the only way to check if the leopard has changed his spots."

"I think that it's a lost battle," said Pat languidly.

"Don't lose heart because of you have failed many times before. It doesn't mean that the failure goes with you hand in hand. How do you know that it is a hundred to one shot if you don't give it one chance again? "

Summer Love

"Do you suggest that I should start over with Graham?"

"You know, it's a big responsibility to give advice. Nobody can tell you that it is suitable for you, if you are not wearing the same shoes. Everybody says what you should do, but the most appropriate. Well, you have asked me something difficult. Anyhow, I will dare to put forward an idea because you are my friend. So, I think that you might have a relationship with Graham, but without setting yourself on him for a while. It sounds silly, but it has to be done in that way until you are quite sure of him. And, about the guy... what is his name?"

"Kenny."

"Well, there is no point in considering a relationship with him, as you have told me that he is quite young, people will talk behind your back when they see you with you."

Kenny's youth was her apprehension that did not let herself any sort of movement. And, it dismayed her soul unfortunately.

"Are you on the phone?"

"Yes."

Summer Love

"What happened? Suddenly, you didn't talk anymore. Is it he who has got you head over heels?"

"No."

"You had better take him away from your mind."

"I don't know what to do," confessed Pat.

"You're the only person who knows. Maybe, you are puzzled but you know what is right for yourself."

"I think so."

A month later, Pat restarted the relationship with her ex-lover without an enormous desire.

IX

One tepid air slid along the place. The roar produced by huge laughter and the elevated tone of voice of the students in their conversations that maintained between themselves involved the atmosphere of the cafeteria. And, in such a timid way, the curly red-haired young man paced up quickly, between the two rows of tables aligned, when a student rising from her seat went to meet him.

"Kenny, are you going?"

"Yes," he answered indecisively.

"Can you give me a lift?"

"Sure... So you keep me company."

The car drove over the black asphalt of longitudinal lane of the motorway at the day's sunset. He was reluctant to get to his destination. So, Kenny tried to lose his way before arriving at central London. His soul did not wish to be caged among the bars of the loneliness.

The youngster made him spring an unknown emotion that it might well go further to be a carnal impulse - despite her provocative clothes. Indeed, it was so. The girl represented something attractive -so he must draw her to his side, but he had never had intimacy with her before.

"To where are we going?" She asked.

"Wherever... Do you mind if we go around?"

"No really... I would like to... Don't you want to drop me off yet?" Leslie told sensually.

"Perhaps," he answered, concealing his real intention.

"Your face speaks for you. You don't want to get home or the place that you're supposed to go. Your eyes are blue and far away."

Summer Love

"It's said that the eyes are the mirrors of the soul. By the way, would you like to have a drink to keep talking?"

The following night, Kenny was lying down with his new friend on a double bed, in a sordid room of a bed and breakfast. In a way, it was an ideal place, which was away from indiscreet and reproachable gazes and contributed to gaiety of the few pleasures of life. The crunch produced by the dots of the screen of the television isolated the shrill cries belonging to a woman, the murmurs' residents who looked for their respective lodgings and some moans of exhilaration from the bedrooms near theirs.

Beams of light came through the half closed door of the bathroom. And, amidst shadows, he slithered his fine fingers over the rough skin of the curved body as his mind was set on the remembrance of Pat -similar to an indelible impression.

Grinding to a halt the strokes of he who was in that moment her lover, the girl demanded. "What are we going to be tomorrow?"

"I don't know. What do you mean?" Kenny asked, shrugging and with knowledge of the meaning of the question.

"What is the point in getting to this if we are not more than friends tomorrow?" Leslie said as a look of annoyance came to her face.

"I think that we shouldn't foresee the events. Wait and see the real thing," he told quietly.

The lad already learnt that the relation would end as his companion had anticipated.

"Do I have to wait?"

"We have to... Drive out the worry from your mind and live this moment."

Summer Love

After his words, Kenny came close to her friend again. His hands madly fondled her body as his pale skin mingled with his lover's black. His lips went downwards and upwards over the body until these reached her face, which was blemished with small pockmark caused by puberty, and lingered on the young's red wine lips.

As the passion dissipated between them, a dreadful bitter sensation possessed the lad. This sentiment came from the most hidden part of his soul, and it had not been recognized before. Now and then, this emotion bloomed as a precious flower in spring. The painful sensation, to have lived a romantic passion with someone whom he did not love, was so heart-sore that it was felt profoundly. That disagreeable emotion came to assure his love for Pat.

He contemplated her naked body, in the mirror of the bathroom, lost in the recollection of Pat. With whom may she be at that precise moment? It was what the lad wondered. She might well be with an unknown person or enjoying her ex-lover's company. Why did she accept him again? He could give only

Summer Love

displeasure to her heart. It was another interrogation that arose in his mind. To the last one was very difficult to figure out inasmuch as his youth had not allowed him to discover yet that people love the others for their vices not for their virtues, so that, when the beloved person shows a good quality the other sees like a benediction fallen from heaven. Kenny would find the answer in the future.

The lad stayed admiring herself without overcoming that sorrow which had struck each fibre of his own heart. Later, in the bed, the lover would await a response to her question. Why did he not accept her? He loved someone else. It may well have been a good explanation. However, Kenny did not deceive himself since his conscience knew perfectly the true cause of that. And, it did not lie on his sentiment for Pat. He did repudiate her due to the others' opinion against that relation. It was the same proceeding as Pat, which he had repulsed. So, what one runs down is prone to do. He would behave like the woman whom he loved.

Summer Love

X

Months went by and Pat had maintained a relationship with the same partner. This once desired union did not gratify all her expectations about it. And, it was not because there was lack of sentiment for him. The emotion given by her lover did not alter with time. However, the discontent was not easy to carry away. The divergences proliferated every day. The causes of those were the different personalities of each one of them. He was not bad, neither good.

Summer Love

Both characters interfered with one another. Graham was on his way and she did the same, but in a contrary direction. There was no an equilibrium in the couple.

Faced with this situation, Pat desired to return the young's unexpected flirting -who was not seen like a boy anymore, but her attention was so drawn to her lover that it did not let her give up to the temptation. As many times, she had the foreboding that the relation might lose, like a flow of water among the fingers of the hands, the illusion that

Summer Love

Kenny once aroused in her heart sprung up again.

Sometimes, she wished to be able to engage herself in a game with them. In that play could be found a fresh emotion, which did not go further to be the person who dominated two or one people rather than to accept to be ruled by someone. Her whim had given the impression of being a stirring experience if Kenny's youth had not wrapped her in fear. That meant her mettle was not tough enough to participate in such a game. Her personality was so faint that it was chained to an unsatisfactory relationship.

Pat wondered what could be done to alter that. From much consideration, she had reached the conviction: "it was better to have a little part of the desired thing - although it was not so agreeable as one had wished- that lost it completely." It was not great her aspiration. How long would Pat keep her certainty? What would she have to bear for it? Those interrogations were removed from her mind as consequence of the knowledge that her disposition did not go further over her own limits.

It was about a year later, when Pat bumped into Kenny by pure chance. The same person that was seen like an adolescent was gazed upon as a man at that moment. He aroused her curiosity once more. Even though, Graham was still interposed between two of them. 'I could split up with one to be with the other', repeated Pat to herself. After all, the election was restricted owing to the obsession that dominated her mettle, which was stronger than any other emotion else.

Summer Love

A battle represented to have those exquisite things that someone else had offered her in a relationship, but she would fight along with Graham to get a sort of perfection in their relation. In such combat, it was not asked her lover's support. Pat always thought for the others.

With respect to Kenny, he was not any longer the lad whom Pat met. After his postgraduate course had finished, he began to deal with a difficult life as it was of an artist. That life was completely different from the others'. In it, there would never be stability although he succeeded. The only possession of such a life was the effort and the failure, but never the success whose property is transient. It was the award. During his way, it would be left behind many things to gain the scorn to his ideas, the others' disdain and the disincentive words from those mouths full of ignorance. Anyhow, it was the life elected by him.

Once, the romance concluded with a young lady -due to lack of interest in her person, he delivered himself up to creative work and non-creative work. The last one was in the mornings practicing his career and the other one at night up to the dawn.

Summer Love

The intensive labour helped to weather his state of depression which burnt him up like a fierce blaze. Such state was a product of the failures of his works which had been put under publisher's considerations, the frustrated attempts to initiate some romantic relations, the dissatisfaction of not getting the desired woman and the unpleasant work that he had to perform every morning. The paramount cause of his depression was not to be in his most enthusiastic occupation. His life had turned into a true disaster.

Summer Love

Frequently, after he left the place of work, in the afternoon's last hours, Kenny would go to any underground station to behold the tracks by where the tube ran. Stood up on the platform, he thought of those people who ended their existence in such a way, without finding out whether it was better to cease with his or not. No one could say a word about it. Although the best was to get rid of a tormented life, his person never dared to pass further the white line painted on the flat raised surface, because there was much fear of pain inside -despite the fact that the agony would be felt for just some seconds. The repudiation of his double life, a common worker at morning and a writer at night, conduced to abandon his post.

    Kenny entirely free dedicated himself to prepare his mind and body to turn back to that repudiable mode of life. In that time, his knowledge was cultivated by reading some classics of the literature and many authors that contributed to give him a particular sort of model to his creations, whilst the principles dictated by metaphysic books were accumulated in his memory.

Summer Love

A mad desire to do the most implausible things and experience those -which people said that were forbidden to those with moral principles, invaded him in the dark night hours. Perhaps, there was no such desire inasmuch as he had gone through them and parted from them by his own will.

From a variety of sentiments, it was considered the existence of just two paths. One that led to an upright life and the other lost inside the depravation. Kenny had reached the conviction that an artist was denied the single choice of one of them, because he should learn to comprehend the human nature in many ways of life.

No choice could be made even though he was set on his feet at the beginning of both, as consequence of being in his lowest spirit the effect was to be despoiled of any sort of emotion. The characters of many books were the inspiration to live the many fascinating sensations that were written in them; however excitement fade away as the cover of the book was shut. And, the senses became blank again.

Summer Love

    Just some metaphysical practices made him achieve to liberate himself from that dreadful frame of mind in which he had remained for many months. As far as the point, it would be so difficult for him to fall in that sombre hole.

XI

"Your obsession doesn't help," said Judith, seated at a table in a café at Covent Garden Market at noon.

"What do you want me to do? I love him. If he were not with me, it would be an obsession. But, Graham is there. In spite of the way he is."

"You think that you aren't. But, as far as you know the relationship doesn't satisfy you. You are always expecting a little thing from him. Don't condition yourself to it. Please, don't fool yourself."

Summer Love

"It's true," Pat muttered. "I leave him. And? I am on my own."

"Sometimes, it's better to be by your own and not tied down," suggested Judith, toying with the straw that was inside the glass.

In a brief silence, Pat contemplated the passers-by that sauntered along and those who ground to a halt to have a look at the exhibitions of the shops.

The friend, into whom she had bumped around the market and invited to have some drink as conversing, had put forward the most drastic solution to choose, so that an annoyed sensation was due not to listen to from those lips a distinct alternative -than to leave the more loved in this world, which meant one of the hardest decision to take in her whole life.

Suddenly, she was invaded by despairing thoughts. In a choleric outburst, she told. "Is there anything better? I don't think so... About a year and half or more, I met a person whose qualities were exceptional. Those any woman dreams to have in her partner. But, nothing is perfect. I was almost eight years older than him.

We can say that he was almost an adolescent."

"Nothing is perfect as you've justly said. If you have something, don't expect to have the other," told Judith, being ironic.

"Should I have taken the risk with Kenny?" demanded Pat, curiously.

"Everything has got its own risk."

"Why is Graham not like him?"

"You told that nothing is perfect."

"But, you have not answered me yet if I should have accepted Kenny," Pat insisted.

"I shall bring two juices and… do you want something to eat? No… When I come back I'll tell you a little story."

Judith trembled with the mild current of air that felt cold because of that the circular blue sunshade did not let the sunbeams warm their bodies up. As she put the beverages on the table, Pat gazed at a shop window that was some distance away from their seats.

Summer Love

The young lady sipped the orange juice before responding to her friend's demand.

"Some time ago, a friend of mine had met a lady, who was almost a patient of his. Well, she was just somebody who approached him to have his medical opinion about a situation, which she was going through. In these occasional meetings, they began to get on together well and, the advice went further. Even though my friend was going out with her, he was with somebody else -who was his fiancée, but the relationship wasn't good. With his new lover, everything was completely different because she pleased him in all senses. However, there was a little problem. She didn't belong to the same class as him. What would his family say? My friend wondered. His family was very important for him. Definitely, they would be against that relationship, and he would have had to face them. In front of this possible situation, he preferred to leave her and kept the relationship with his fiancée. His choice was so tough and for the other woman that she had to go to a shrinker... What about my friend and his fiancée? Six months later, after the wedding, they got divorced. At the moment, he regrets having taking such a decision, on terms of having considered the others' opinion. The worst, there were no obstacles such as economics that stopped him from breaking up any relation with his family, neither religious principle that forbade him to marry her. My friend thinks that life will give him another chance to meet someone who pleases him as that woman did. He is wrong. An opportunity comes along just once."

"How are you going to think that there is comparison between me and your thick friend," reproved Pat, frowning.

"He is not a thick as you call him. My friend is a learned man. But, he conducted as if he had been an idiot. However, anybody can do the same. Besides, there is just one step from intelligence to stupidity."

"For you, everything is very easy because you see it from outside. You pulled off getting a husband, so you have now solution for all kind of problems."

"Don't be silly. That doesn't mean you get rid of trouble. These turn to be more complicated. Your partner got his own personality, and he has things you wish he didn't have, but you have to accept them because the good traits are more than the bad ones. You don't want to leave your boyfriend since you say that you are head over heels in love with him, and there is nobody perfect. In fact, that kind of person doesn't exist, but there are men better than Graham. Try to find someone who is near the kind of man you dream," asserted Judith, getting upset.

    She maintained herself in silence.

"Do as you want! Pardon me, if my words have bothered you."

"Don't mind."

"See you later," said Pat's friend, arising from her chair at the table.

Her friend's thickset figure lost between the flock that were marching along the passage, whilst her mind was in deep meditation. It had broken out a war of recommendations in which each one differed with another. Who had suggested the best? Her heart inclined to believe that it had been her closest friend who knew perfectly well her personality, so that she would not ask a third opinion.

Summer Love

Pat got up and joining the others began to make her way. She was much more tranquil on account of having taken a decision just some moments ago. It was paramount in her life. Now hope enraptured her soul, which was fortified by Ravel's bolero played by young musicians downstairs. A smile drew over her lips -cheering her countenance up, when her eyes laid on a red-haired man, whose green carriage was stopped behind him. The shabby tall trickster was performing his act to sell his goods at the entrance of the south hall.

Summer Love

The sun seemed to have a more intense brightness that any day before. Again, everything turned to have a sparkling colour. It was amazing as the fear melted away and emanated a desire to reach happiness at her partner's side.

XII

Some months had gone by since the chat with her friend at the market.

At dusk, on a summer day, reddish shafts were coloured over the hollowed light blue canvas. Driving through the streets, Pat pulled in the half way of one.

"I'll see you tomorrow?"

"Certainly... I must update some work tonight."

"All right... Will you pick me up?"

"Yes. I'll call you before," Graham said, getting out of the car.

As her boyfriend entered the building, Pat drove off. When she was in the middle on her way, she saw a key ring left on the front passenger seat. However, she didn't turn back. So, Pat had now an excuse to see him tonight.

At nine o' clock in the evening, Pat went to her boyfriend's home. On arrival, she opened every door herself with the keys that she had in her hand. As she went inside the apartment, she pronounced with a soft voice.

"Graham."

Summer Love

There was no response to her call. Perhaps, his partner was asleep; she had considered it. A low sound of music came from his bedroom, so Pat went upstairs.

"Graham!" His name broke from her lips as she was startled.

The bottle of wine that she had brought fell to the ground. Being not able to say any word, Pat left the place quickly. He rushed to stop her but the contact of his bare feet with the scattered sharp fragments of glass impeded him to carry on.

A bitter sensation had hurt her soul. The thing she most desired was to forget that disagreeable situation. She got lost in the streets before she went off London. The dark lanes of the motorway led her to the south.

The firmament was adorned with luminous points. Underneath, Pat lonely sauntered along a promenade in order to meditate. She had behaved foolishly. All her considerations were completely wrong. In fact, these had come from a mad reasoning as a consequence of one destructive sentiment, as obsession was. Pat had followed her close friend's advice even though it was not right, because this proceeded from the same decision

Summer Love

that Kate would have taken if she had been before the choice. At the beginning, the recommendation was not so absurd until the union turned to be thorny.

At that moment, the recollection of seeing her lover lying on the bed with a colleague of hers was so agonizing that it would be impossible to get rid of it. Although that person was not a friend, she was just someone for whom Pat felt some affection when each began to know the other. The betrayal was not so heart-rending as the fact that he was cheating on her with that woman. She had accepted that sort of relation whose bases were not sustained in respect. Pat had fallen so low. An inferiority complex bound her like a chained man dumped into the sea.

Her eyes reposed over the dark seawaters meanwhile some interrogations about tomorrow crossed her mind. There was no response, neither even foreboding. Already, her fate was not so important for herself.

At the brake of dawn, Pat drove off the town.

XIII

From that moment, Pat sunk herself into a profound melancholy. The forces that emerged from her soul to bear the burden that represented the relationship had been worthless because of having conditioned herself to tolerate unbearable situations for nothing. Even the most intense effort could not avoid the collapse. The sentimental product of the deception arose inside her conducing to despoil of any interest about life. This emotion would possess her for long time.

Pat may have healed those wounds through the maddest adventures or with the invention of one delight. A pleasure might be Kenny. However, she was rather worn out with the first and not ready yet for the second. In many times before, she had walked along the path of rarest experience to cure severe hurts or deepen them. To those gashes that had not healed up with thrilling experiences, time had been responsible for anointing a sort of oil upon them. And, the indifference with which the past is seen was the ointment applied over her lacerated soul. One way or another, she foresaw that days would be incapable of taking away the distressing remembrances from her mind.

In mysterious nights, where thousands of ideas haunted her thought -leaving without peace to her sleep, came along the figure of the young man in her memories. A sort of agitation emerged from her inner part that faded away completely by the morning light so as to appear at the twenty-third hour again. On those hours of the profound disturbance,

Summer Love

Pat attempted to dial his number but the fear experienced turned her fingers clumsy and made her desist from such intention.

After a certain time, in which she was parted from social life and was self-absorbed as if she had been inside a protecting shell against outer actions, she paid the proper attention to the outside world. In that epoch, her mood was not characterized to attend the gatherings to which she had been invited with the same companion. Her tastes inclined to a variety of male friends in order not to be tempted by the fancy that someone

Summer Love

may give her and found herself dominated by one man. The shamefacedness was disguised with a gesture to conceal it. Pat had a new personality or assumed that attitude - which was dreamt to possess- to face up to life.

On a Sunday's afternoon, after having lost herself in Van Gogh's impressionism, where her eyes drifted upon the ochre disks and yellow petals of the 'Sunflowers' (which represents hope and friendship), and her soul was ecstatic by the wavy light coloured lines of the painting 'A Wheatfield With Cypresses', Pat was seated at a table in the café of the National Art Gallery.

Her view passed carelessly around the place until they fixed on the slim figure of a woman who was considerably tall and her black hair was loose up to the back. The person's shape reminded her of whom was once her close friend. Anyhow, Pat was not able to recognize who it was until the lady turned around. The agate eyes and the branded lines descending from each side of the nostrils as far as the chin and the untidy look revealed her identity.

"Excuse me for a moment, Brian. I'd like to greet a friend of mine."

'Who was the person that accompanied her friend?' It was the question that she was wondering as paced up to them.

"Hi! How are you?"

"Fine... Since you left the hospital I've hardly ever bumped into you."

"A little busy at the moment... That's all." Kate introduced her friend. "By the way, this is Ron."

"Pat, glad to meet you," she said, astounded.

Summer Love

"Ron."

"Would you excuse us for a moment, Ronny? I need to ask Kate something. Women's things, you know."

"Sure."

"Well, I'll be with you in a minute," Kate told.

"This is your boyfriend, isn't he?" She demanded, annoyed.

"Well, I just go out with him."

"But, he's almost an adolescent! You should be older than him by about ten or twelve years."

"And...? I like him. I don't mind his age. The important thing here is personality."

"Have you changed your opinion?" Pat asked, biting her lip.

"What?" Kate was amazed at the question as turning around her sight when someone bowled her.

"Wasn't it you who advised me that I shouldn't make a fuss over Kenny by his youth? I'm barely older than him… And, you told me that our relationship would go nowhere."

"Well, I did it 'cause you wished to be told so. I didn't do more than that. You said that he seemed to be your son and you were afraid of his youth. Isn't it?" She retorted. "Besides, you really cared about others' opinion. What did you want me to tell you?"

"And, you don't care about people?"

"No, I live my life as I please. My life doesn't have to do with anyone."

Those suggestible words once uttered had led her life inasmuch as having coming from her friend. The cause of her anger was not due to the fact that Kate had preached without proper example or did not dare to do the same as her. Pat's blood boiled as a consequence her judgment did not exercise influence on the others in the least.

XIV

In the turquoise sky, little clouds, of divers forms delineated silhouettes of heavenly cities and the rarest birds, drifted through the firmament. The sun lit up all with its yellowish light. And, the wind was far away from there.

She strolled over the pebbles towards the man who was abstracted from everything that was around him.

"Busy?"

"No." He was awestruck. "What a surprise!"

Pat sat down by him.

"What can I say, Kenny?"

He burst out when she called him for short.

"No more Kenny. From now on, my full name Kennangh, please."

"Pardon me."

"So, what are you doing here?"

"The sun, the sea and…"

"And...?" Kennangh asked.

"You know it very well."

"I don't really know," said he, as if the reason were unknown to him.

"Don't be silly! You know it very well. Anyway, I'll tell you because I haven't come here to waste my time like a teenager keeping myself going around what I want. The reason for being here is you."

"Quite frank… But, why…?"

"Should there be a reason?"

"So, you have one… What about me? Maybe, I am not interested in you anymore."

"Why?" Pat demanded, in fear.

"Do you want the boy or the man?" He asked.

"Don't try to change the subject here, please."

"Well, I am not fond of any relationship for the moment. I'm just focused on what I want."

"And, what do you want?"

"Be an established author." Kennangh added. "I have to work hard to be a one. And, I'll do anything for it."

"Anything means a lot."

"No doubt about it."

"Where is the guy who was going to struggle against adversity until it was defeated? I remember being told that he has been tempted by unfair actions but he never gave up to them. Did I happen to have met someone else? I thought that it was you when I recognized just some minutes ago. But, I was wrong, was I?"

The last question made him uneasy.

"You taught me to be so. Weren't you who paraphrased about people's morality and the nature of actions? 'Anything that has a bad beginning will have a bad end.' You couldn't leave moral principles or scruples at one side. 'Everything comes and goes.' What happened with all that? Who of the two of us told first?"

"Certainly, it was me who turned her back against all my words.

Summer Love

Let me tell you something that is so real as life itself -I heard it once. Those who run down something is 'cause they are tired of doing it. I've been one and made mistakes. I can't deny it. Everything's gone wrong. Pleased?"

"No, I am not."

"I got the man. I noticed when I saw you. You are not the same one. Perhaps, 'cause of there are no little curls in your hair anymore. But now, I know that I perceived something different. And, it was inside you. You are no longer a teenager. Well, you weren't when I met you. At that time, my eyes watched a touch of innocence in you, but they can't see it now. What's the matter with you? Why did you change?"

"Nothing... I just go for what I want. And, morality won't be a great help. Besides, I'm concentrated on living too. No time to miss anything."

"What to live, my boy... what is supposed to be forbidden?"

"Perhaps," Kennangh told ironically.

"Your mind says nothing about?"

"No at all." He added. "But, you haven't felt any desire for what is banned?"

"Yes, I have." Pat heaved a sigh. "But, I want to forget it now."

He had noticed her sadness.

"Have I still a place in your life?" She asked lastly.

Kennangh laid his eyes over the broad sea.

"You should have… At least, you meant one emotion to live. Anyway, the whole thing is like a story that has a good storyline in spite of being badly written. So, I don't know if I can get rid myself of the sour."

Summer Love

Unpleasantness was between them.

"You can't get rid of it?"

"Don't be silly! I can"

"Then, you mean that there is still a place?"

"Yes."

XV

From the seed that was sown before, a relationship blossomed. The union might be for their lifetime. For a long time, Pat lived one of the most pleasant relations in her life. He gave her those smallest and biggest details that enlivened any union –tokens of affection always expected from her partner and never offered her in previous relationships. Kennangh's attention to her person was endless, the love came from him was unique, the communication turned him into more than a lover, and the respect which he had for his partner made her insides flourish with a sort of gratification that enraptured all her soul. Sometimes, Pat censured herself for the fact of having left the young man for stupid ideas. Nevertheless, her reproach disappeared as she was by his side.

As time went by, Pat thought about matrimony. However, it was not under her partner's consideration. It was such a strange life! Before she could not imagine tying her life to Kennangh's. Now, her mind dreamt about it daily.

Summer Love

In that period, his life continued being double. In the mornings, he used to work as an executive in the offices of an imposing edifice where there were financial, commercial and service firms, and at nights, he delivered himself up to write those ideas that came to his imagination in a small studio in his home until the hours of darkness wore away. From the product of his non-creative work, he managed to obtain enough funds to go through an edition of his work. At the beginning, the book did not have any acceptance whatsoever, but as the editor along with the writer

Summer Love

promoted the run, fruitful results were achieved. The adversity began to be defeated. Suddenly, his double life would have an end.

The future presented itself as promising -there was not a doubt of it.

XVI

The mellow susurrus of the strike of the waves against the rocks delighted his ears. Kennangh was standing up in front of the shutter contemplating the splendour of the last quarter over the peaceful waters of the coast. The mild current of air that came in covered all his nude figure.

His conscience deliberated about how to make known an important resolution to his partner.

However, he couldn't summon up the courage to pronounce those words.

"It's a wonderful place, isn't it? I wish we lived here... I want you to be with me for good," said Pat, throwing her arms around him.

"Yes, this place is marvellous... I like Jamaica."

"Why are you sad?"

"Well, I think that it is about time to tell you."

"What?"

"Pat, I am travelling after we go back."

"What is the problem...? I already miss you."

"It is not what you think," Kennangh told, with a melancholic tone in his voice.

"Explain, please."

"I'm going to America. I have got an opportunity to work on a film."

"It would be great there."

"I'm settling down there," he announced.

"What is it?"

Kennangh leant his head on the vertical edge of the shutter while the agony perturbed his heart and his words came out being gasped.

"I am going on my own."

"And... I?" She demanded wryly.

"You...? You will stay in England," said he, recovering his composure.

Pat flushed and with her eyes blazing with cholera pulled herself away.

"What... are you telling me that you are leaving me for an offer?"

Turning his look around, Kennangh nodded.

"Why... have I done anything wrong?" She added. "You don't love me anymore?"

"I love you. And, you don't have an idea how much I do. But, I don't want to take any risk."

Summer Love

"I don't understand. What risk...?"

"I won't pass on this opportunity. It's big for me. Your career and friends mattered a lot yesterday."

"And...?"

Pulling a funny face, he answered. "And, you didn't care about Kenny."

"I know it. But, you don't have a clue about what I went through," confessed Pat, as tears welled up in her eyes.

"I still remember how difficult was to make you forget him. In our early days, I always thought that you would run to him again. And, I knew that you would… In spite of having in mind all it was his fancy. However, I can't tell if you hold something for him now."

"Your lips can't say it 'cause you know well who I love. But, your stupidity doesn't let you accept it."

"As I told you once, a good storyline but badly written. It was you who dared me to accept you! And, I didn't know if it was love or just to have what I didn't. At any rate, whatever it was has given up to my ideas. Anyway, if you had loved me, someone else's opinions would have not weighed on your decisions."

"I love you. And, if I took into account someone else's comment it was for the worst," she retorted.

"Your indifference was so painful."

"I know I hurt you."

"But, I don't want to hurt you," Kennangh told, with a lump in his throat.

"Please, stay with me."

"Why you didn't love me when I did?"

Summer Love

"I came into your life too late?" Pat asked, as tears were running down her cheeks.

"No, you didn't. You came along at the right moment, but you left me for later on. In this life, there's just today and no tomorrow. Future doesn't exist. And, when it comes it is already present. So, don't worry about tomorrow."

"Why do you say that?"

"For those things that you thought and didn't let you be with me when I met you for first time."

Summer Love

Taking his hand, she invited him. "Let's make love, Kenny... Love me."

"I love you."

"So do I," said Pat.

Ingram Content Group UK Ltd.
Milton Keynes UK
UKHW010808190623
423681UK00015B/581